THE MAGICAL NIGHTMARES

JACK PARKER

Contents

Prologue

"It's Gary, Anyone copy?". "It's Finn. I copy. What happened?". "Can you give me tomorrow's test notes? Over".

"What didn't you have the notes for tomorrow's test? Never mind, I'm coming in a bit. Over". "Thanks man".

Gary is so irresponsible. I got in the car and went to Garys. "Here... here you go." I gave Gary a book. "What? You are not doing?". "I've already read everything".

"How?" Gary stares at me. "You want it or what?".

"Sorry, sorry... Tomorrow is our last exams. Any plans after that?" Gary asked. "First, let's give the tests and then we'll figure out what to do". "What happened to Henry? Have you spoken with him? He didn't respond," said Gary.

"Yes, perhaps he is preparing for the tomorrow's test". "See you in school tomorrow," I told Gary. "Bye... and thanks for this" Gary smiled.

In the morning walking to school, I met Henry "Hey, good morning" Henry said. "Good morning. Today is our last day at school. Feeling kinda sad about that". "Yes, so am I. We've been together since the second or third unit, haven't we? Said Henry. "Yes, probably second".

When we arrived at the school, Gary was there. He looked at us with joy in his face, as today is our last test. "You look so happy" Henry said Gary. "Absolutely, anybody can tell by looking at his face," I said.

Henry was in his classroom, Gary and I were walking to ours. While walking in the hallway, Naysa was standing outside her classroom. "Finn, go tell her Best of luck..." Gary said. "No...". "She saw you, tell her. You're not a pussy, are you?".

"Absolutely not". "Then, go for it, Tiger".

I walked to Naysa and said "Good luck for today's exam" and immediately moved into my classroom and sat down. *What did I do. I didn't even give her a chance to wish me back.*

I have not introduced myself, right? I am Finn Anderson, I just finished my High-school, to be specific, I am not good at studies, or am I? That two stupid is my friends, Gary Adams and Henry Wilson. Gary's father is very rich and having a big house and Henry was just like me living in an old town building.

CHAPTER ONE

COINCIDENCE?

Today is May Sixth, 1969. "Hey Finn" Stacy and her friends waved at me. "Hey Girls". The corridor was filled with students, everyone was happy. I walked out of the school with my friends.

"At last, it's over, we're free now," said Gary. "Yes, we are free now" I agreed. "So where are we headed?" asked Gary. "We should go and eat something first and after that we should go to the paradise" I replied. "Paradise? You mean heaven. We had to die for that. No, no, you're good to go."

"What the heck... dude. I mean the game store, to play the arcade games" I hit Gary's head. "Take it easy... just kidding. What's the matter with him? He is so quiet. It's not normal," Gary whispered into my ear.

"What happened, your paper wasn't good?" I asked Henry, he seemed afraid. "No, it's just dogs". "What dogs? Are you afraid of dogs?" Gary asked. "No, I just thought the dogs were chasing us." Henry replied. "Relax, no one is chasing us." I spoke.

We marched to a café near Gary's house. We had a meal and were walking to Gary's house. Gary needs to grab his stuff.

As walking to Gary's house, Henry was looking here and there as he was sure that a group of dogs was about to chase us. "Don't be afraid Henry there are no dogs in Gary's area" I said confidently. "What makes you so sure?".

"I know this area; I always go by this road back home". "But this road takes longer to get to your house than the town road," said Henry. "I know, I know why," Gary said as he laid his hand on my shoulder. "Why tell me, why?"

We arrived at Gary's house, Henry and I were waiting for Gary to show up. "Let's go" Gary came running. After strolling for 5 minutes "Why are we even on foot? We can drive there" Henry said. "Yes, we can but, Finn's home is away and my car was given to fix" Gary responded. "Woohoo... this is new. You have given your car for repair. Why don't you buy another one?" I mocked Gary. "Except that is a **MUSTANG SHELBY GT 350** 1968 with 302 cubic engine v8 and the 335 horsepower" Gary replied. "Yeah man, I know".

We made it to the store and Henry was relieved no dogs were coming for us. "What should we play today?" Henry asked.

Then we played for a couple of hours and left the store. "What should we do now? Where should we go?" Gary asked. "We must now go home!" said Henry. "You're still scared of dogs, aren't you?" We should go to the beach side to see the sun-set, it's almost time" I grabbed Henry's shoulder and started walking.

We had found a place in the city, from where the sunset seems perfectly beautiful. We got there and sat. The sunset was so beautiful that it seems like we were looking through the gates of heaven. "It's magnificent!" Henry exclaimed. "Yes man" I replied.

"We should probably get going now, it's dark," said Henry. It was dark and we were all headed home.

Henry said, "Please, Finn, come walk with me to the house, my house is just in your way". "Don't be afraid of dogs Henry, you're a grown-up boy". "Maybe he is not" Gary said breezily "He is a pussy". "Yes... pussies are afraid of dogs" Gary and I shrieked with laughter. "Let's not laugh at him, he's really afraid, let's go. See you Gary" I said. "See YA..."

We were walking to our home and reached without being chased by any dog as it seems there was no dog in the town, but I had seen some dogs near the town's garden area.

I ate my dinner and entered the bedroom. *It's bedtime, I'll sleep until tomorrow evening. I didn't get much sleep this week. Why am I talking to myself.*

TRING TRING TRING!! TRING TRING TRING!!

It's the telephone it is beeping so loud in the middle of the night. *Why gary is calling?* I pick up the phone "Hey come to Henry's house it's an emergency his mother has called us!" before I could even ask what happened Gary hung-up.

It was 1 in the morning. I sneaked out because I don't want to wake my mom and dad. I took the car, still I am not qualified to ride a car. I arrived at Henry's house and there Gary and Henry's mother were talking. *She's a beauty.*

They told me that Henry has not come home since 11 o'clock. He went to the town store to pick up some ice cream. *Should I call her aunty or mom, no no.* "Don't worry Ms. Wilson, we will go find Henry" I told unconsciously.

We sat in the car and drove slowly to the city. "The police of our town are terrible, they told Ms. Wilson he'll be back, he's big enough to be on his own," said Gary. "What do you think he's doing?" I wondered. "I have no idea! I wonder where is he, he is a lazy person" Gary said.

Yes, that's for sure he is. He didn't even have a dad. He said that his parents got divorced when he was three years old. Who can give divorce to such a beautiful lady.

"What are you thinking, keep your eyes on the road," said Gary, looking at me in an odd way. "Yes... Yes...." I grilled "Did she check the house? Maybe he is sleeping in the house only, he never wakes up this late". "She told me she checked and she even gave me his photo if anyone asked" Gary replied recalling his conversation with Ms. Wilson.

The road of the city is empty. Not a single soul is awakened here, despite the fact that the ice cream shop was still open. We went into the shop and asked the owner if he had seen Henry by showing his picture. He thoughtfully said "Yes, this boy came at around 11:30 and bought some ice creams and left".

"So, he came here, but didn't reach home" Gary said in an intriguing way. "Thank you, mister..." I said as I left. "We should go through this route; we will find out where he is" I told Gary. *What would be the reason behind Henry's absence.*

We were inspecting everything on the way. I saw a white bag and in the bag ice cream were spilled. There was a shoe beside the bag. "See, that's Henry's shoe, right? At 4 o'clock. It's the same as Henry's shoes" I said terrorize, pointing my finger at the bag. "It looks similar" Gary said.

It was a huge abandoned bungalow. I parked the car. "Let's go inside!!" I said panicking. The door of the house was locked. There was a big backyard. We were walking tremulously. We heard a noise. "We should leave I'm not getting good vibes here" Gary said moving backwards.

We again hear that noise; it was like someone snoring loudly. I told Gary to go and check it one time. That was

Henry, sleeping peacefully on the big broken slide in the backyard. *I wonder how he got there.* We were relaxed as it was not any monsters or ghosts who were making those noises.

"Henry, wake up buddy. Henry" I bawled. We woke him up and asked him what happened. He didn't respond, though. He said that he will tell everything tomorrow. Henry wants to sleep, so we drop him off at his house first and I drop Gary off. *What will the reason. Why didn't he say anything? Ugh… It's already four in the morning and I am very tired.*

The minute I woke up, I showered and asked Gary to come to Henry's. Today is May Seventh. I reached Henry's house, I knock, and Ms. Wilson opens the door. *Even today she is looking so pretty. Is it wrong to think of my friend's mother that she's beautiful?*

"Good morning, Ms. Wilson, is everything okay?" I sincerely asked. "Yeah, last night was just unpleasant."

I walked into Henry's room and a minute later Gary arrived. "Now, would you tell us what took place last night? We were tensed" I said abruptly. "I'm going to say something that you will not believe. Yesterday I dreamt that I was being chased by a group of dogs, and it happened"

"What are you saying, we are asking you the reason behind your disappearance, how did you end up sleeping on that big broken slide of an abandoned house?" I again asked angrily.

Henry said subtly "While walking back to home from the ice cream store, the dog chased me and I ran into the old house and somehow I managed to climb the slide, I hold there till the dogs go and while waiting them to leave, I slept there only".

"Wait, that's not true, isn't it?" said Gary mysteriously, with his eyes wide open. "He's telling the truth; his shoes and the ice cream bag were on the floor," I said without knowing. "Yes, that's what happened". "Maybe it's all just a coincidence or happened because you thing that will happen" I said.

"Now you are having magical dreams" Gary said whilst eating chips. "It was more like a nightmare," I told him. "Coincidentally, I don't think so, did you have a dream last night?" asked Gary enthusiastically. "No, last night I didn't," said Henry.

Is there any sense about what they are talking? There's no such thing as magical dreams or nightmares. "All right, let's forget about it and enjoy... our exams are over," I said without wanting to say forget. "Well then we should go and play arcade games" Gary said.

CHAPTER TWO

THE ANCIENT PILLOW.

We were planning on taking a picnic somewhere. Henry and I are at Gary's and we were fed up playing the same games. We are staying at Gary's house for 2 days as his parents were going out of town.

Today is eleventh and I still wonder about that magical dream what Henry has told. "Did anything happen after that nightmare came true, any other dream?" Gary asked while sitting on the lounger next to Henry. "No, nothing after that day, even I had a dream that I was in the house of chocolates, but nothing happened, perhaps Finn was right" Henry replied. "See told YA..." I said wondering. *So that was just coincidence.*

"I have heard that sometimes not all dreams are realized, but some. My grandpa used to tell me stories about it" Henry said. "I believe too" Gary agreed with Henry. *They are just small children talking about stories.*

"So... what should we do today, we have all night we should do something," I said, sitting between them as I lay my hands on the shoulder of Gary and Henry. "I think we should watch movies tonight, like a scary movie with popcorns," Gary said in the tone that he's the ghost.

ls that the way ghosts talk? I have never heard one. "Yeah, we should watch at midnight to be specific" I spoke.

"I'm afraid of all these movies" Henry cried. "Don't worry, nothing will happen" Gary said. Then we talked about our past and time went by and it was almost midnight.

"It's midnight, let's start the movie, I'm excited" Gary said while turning on the TV. After 2 hours of continuously watching the movie, barely 4-5 times the ghost appeared in the movie, there was nothing to be afraid of this movie. Though Henry was so petrified. "See nothing happened" Gary told Henry. "The movie was not that scary" I said while eating popcorn.

After watching we all went into Gary's bedroom, he has a large bed on which 3-4 people can sleep comfortably. Henry has brought his old pillow with him. "Your pillow is so antique" I told Henry, taking his pillow. "Yeah, it was my grandpa's pillow, he gave it to me" Henry said.

"So, are you sleeping with that pillow?" said Gary while thinking something. "Yes, that's why I bring it with me" Henry replied. "Since when have you ever used that pillow?" Gary asked Henry. "Only a few days, my mother cleaned the storeroom over there, I got this pillow". "The day you slept with this pillow when this nightmare happened?" Gary asked. "Yes, after that my mom washed it as it was so filthy" Henry replied.

What is going on inside Gary's head. "That's why the chocolate dream never came true because you slept without that pillow!" Gary said with excitement. "What...? Now you are saying that the ancient pillow is magical? " I inquired with perplexity.

"Think Finn, when he slept with that pillow, his dream became his reality, but when he didn't nothing happened" Gary said while seeing the pillow carefully. Henry was listening gingerly with his eyes wide open. "No... there's nothing magical about this antique pillow, it all just happens in the stories" I argued.

"All right, we'll find out, Henry, you're going to sleep with that ancient pillow today". Sometimes Gary is an eight-year-old kid. " I'm sleeping with this pillow only, and don't call it ancient pillow, it's from my grandfather" Henry cried.

What...? I'm unable to process this. Does Henry really have an ancient magical pillow, that fulfills the dreams? Whatever... let's sleep.

I woke up before Gary and Henry and was still thinking about the magical pillow and dreams. Its May Twelfth. I cleaned my teeth and had a cold shower. Gary was also awake; he was in the bathroom. Henry was still sleepin'. *I wonder what is he dreaming about.*

After Henry woke up, Gary ran to him and asked, "Did you dream anything?". "I don't remember, I'll tell you when I recall it" Henry said memorizing. As after Henry moves towards the bathroom. "You really believe in fairy tales and magic?" I asked Gary.

"It's not a fairy tale, but yes... of course I believe in magic," Gary answered. Henry was murmuring something in the bathroom. He was trying to recollect his memory during the shower.

Like when Henry came out Gary said "Recalled something?". "No, nothing," said Henry in a tone of disguise.

"What...? Nothing? Not a single thing. But you did dream something... right?" Gary keeps on interrogating Henry.

"Cooldown... dreams do not come true in real life!!" I cried aloud.

Gary was really an 8 years old child. Gary's father called him and said there will be no power in the area from 6 PM to 8 PM as some work is going on in the city.

"I think we should go visit the novel places in the city as there will be no power here" I said. Both of them agree in saying, "Hmmm...". *What's going on in their heads?*

It's afternoon, we are in the big pool enjoying. "Gary you should talk about our plans to visit that resort to your father, as he knows the owner of the resort" I told Gary while drinking orange juice in a wine glass. "I will definitely talk to him about that once he comes".

After that, I left as my mom called me and told me to bring vegetables from the shop.

As I was walking towards the store, I saw Ms. Wilson going somewhere. *She was too young to be Henry's mom.* I shouted and waved "Hey Ms. Wilson, Good evening, ". She stopped as I ran to her "Good evening Finn, are you going to buy vegetables?". I nodded my head. "All right, let's walk together, " She said.

You are looking beautiful, should I say that or not. What will she think?

She asked, "You're staying at Gary's house, right?". "Yes, but mom had given me the job of buying veggies for her."

"Wait... give me the list, I'll buy it and give it to your mother, I hadn't met her for a while...". *She is so sweet.*

"You sure about that?". "Yes, definitely you go, have fun at Gary's." She responded. "No, let me give you some company up to the shop, then I'll go."

"You're such a sweet boy," She said. I was blushing "Thanks". "Do you believe in fairy tales and magic?" I asked her

"No... I do not, do you?" She spoke. But her face said otherwise, as if she was scared of something. "No, no... I'm not buying it either". "And where is this question coming from?" she asked. "No, nothing, I saw a book about it". *WTF... that was a lie.*

We reached the store and bought the vegetables and then I left.

As it was 5:30 PM, Gary and Henry were waiting for me. We decided to go ice skating first, then a place to dine. Gary said, "I have 3-4 ice skates, but we have to find it, or they're gonna charge more for ice skates".

"We should do a thing, Henry you should go purchase the tickets, me and Gary will drive Immediately when we get the ice skates" I spoke.

Both agreed. Henry left and we were finding the skates in the store room. The storeroom was so big and was full of items inside. I find the skates under the stairwell in the storeroom. We heard some noise upstairs.

We took 3 pairs of skates and was leaving then Gary said "That dummy left his walkie here only". We took his walkie, and left.

We made it, but Henry wasn't here, we were scared about what happened to him now. "What should we do now? Should we call the cops? Should we tell Ms. Wilson? Gary said anxiously. I pulled my walkie-talkie out of my bag "He's just gonna be here somewhere, we should find him",

"Hello Henry, Do you copy?..." I spoke on my walkie. "But his walkie talkie is with me... here, he forgot to take". We searched all over the place, but there was no sign of Henry. It's about 2 hours since Henry was missing. How can he always end up missing.

"What should we do? What should we do now? " Gary frightened.

We called the cops and told them about Henry. They told us to meet them at Gary's house. "Did you see him move out of your house?" I asked Gary. "No... but he told us that he is going, right?". "We should look at your place first"

Gary opened the door and we saw Henry seated on the floor, he looked terrified. *What the fuck... He was all by himself in the house and there was no electricity in the area.* "What happened...? Are you cryin'?" I asked Henry. No, I was so scared that everything was dark. No one was there" Henry replied while sitting on the chair.

Henry explained that when we were finding the skates, he came back to get his wallet from Gary's room and was not able to find his walkie in the dark. "We heard something, but we weren't certain," I said.

"The back door is always open, you can come out from that door." Gary said. "I did not know that; how am I supposed to know that. I was alone and the power was gone," Henry said as he pulled the water bottle from the fridge.

"All right... let's just forget that. We called the cops, Gary, what are we supposed to tell them?" I asked.

Afterwards, the cops came and entered the house. We all overstated things because it was our own mistake. The officer understands and left.

"Henry, are you all-right? We thought you were kidnapped" I spoke. "I'm all right, just I have a dread of dark" Henry said in agitation.

"Have you dreamt about that...? Trapped inside the house in the dark all alone" Gary asked. Henry didn't say anything, maybe because he was stunned or hiding something. "We should now go to a restaurant to eat something, I'm so hungry," I said.

Why didn't he says something. Did he actually dream about it? Did he really have a magical ancient pillow that fulfills dreams? Why there are so many questions in my mind.

CHAPTER THREE

FANTASY.

We slept after that and now we have no idea what we should or shouldn't do? Last night, Henry slept without that pillow. "Yesterday, I didn't dream a thing," said Henry. We were all still under a lot of stress.

"We should go to the café next door," I said, forcing both of them to stand up. "Yeah..." Gary said.

We walked to a cafe named Deux Cafe. "What you will have... I could use a mocha with pasta" I said while sitting on the table. "Me as well..." said Henry. "I'll take a latte," said Gary. "I'll give the order, you guys carry on..." I said as I was heading to the counter to give orders.

"We should definitely talk to somebody," I muttered, but nobody had heard that. "I don't believe in this ancient magical pillow thing, if there is something you should definitely throw that pillow away" I argued.

"It's not ancient!! And it's my grandpa's I'm not going to throw it!" Henry cried. Our order came and the waiter helped us.

"You are good right? Do you want to discuss it with your mom?" I asked Henry about it, holding the mug. "No... I'm fine," said Henry, but he was afraid anyway.

"But you don't look alright," said Gary. "I really don't believe in this whole magical, fairy-tale thing," I said while eating pasta.

"I don't know what the hell's going on," Henry said. "We can do one thing if we want to ascertain the truth" Gary said confidently. "What" we both said contemporaneously. "We should use the magical pillow, you know, me and Finn".

"That's your plan; I beg to differ," I cried. "Just once, it will help to discover the actual truth" Gary asked. "Alright, just once". Henry was listening all this faintly.

"We didn't even ask Henry; can we borrow your pillow?" I asked. "Well, you're my buddies so you can" Henry said.

After that we had our meal and then we walked back to Gary's. Gary's parents are back from their trip and we need to get back to our place.

From May Thirteen till May Sixteenth, we use it 2-2 times while sleeping, but we haven't dreamed a single thing.

Up until the seventeenth, Gary dreamt he drove a super car, Ferrari. We three were gathered in the town garden.

He's rich, which is maybe why his dreams were so high class. I didn't even dream of riding a Mustang. I have no doubt that was not going to happen. This wasn't his dream, it was his fantasy.

"What do you think Finn, will this happen or not?" Gary asked. "No, that's not going to happen, and what of the car what model was it?" I asked.

Well, he doesn't know I have a thing for cars and especially supercars. "Model...? I Dunno. But it was the latest of all" Gary said with that glitter in his eyes. "So, you dreamt about the **Ferrari 365 GT** or **super-fast** or **GTS**?" I asked

He didn't answer, it was like he didn't grasp what I had just said.

The entire day just passed by, but still Gary was waiting for some miracle to happen so that he can ride a 'Ferrari'. "Stop waiting for some *'Merveille'* to happen" I said. "What...? Which way? " Henry asked misleadingly.

"No Henry there is no way it's *'Merveille,'* in English it's like some kind of wonder or miracle" Gary said. "You both know French, that's good I can only speak one language" Henry told in a sorrowful manner.

"It's twelve in the morning, now we should go home and sleep," I said. "Yes, Finn is correct..." Henry agreed. Then we made our way home.

Nothing took place yesterday. There was nothing magical. That one dream was just coincidence or fate. If the pillow is a magical, something would have happened but nothing. What do you think Finn? 'Why am I asking questions to myself?'

"Hey Finn, Do you copy?" Walkie spoke. No, it wasn't walkie, it's Gary. "It's Finn, I copy. Over" I replied. "What are you doing? Over". "Nothing, was listening music. Over"

"Where is Henry? Henry, do you copy? " I asked. "It's Henry, over". "There he is, meet me at the garden. Over" Gary said. "What for? Over" I asked, he didn't reply. *WTF now.*

I took my car and drove to Henry and then drove to the garden. I saw Gary standing outside the garden. We stepped outside the car "What happened? Why did you call". "Nothing, just feeling lonely at home" Gary smirked. I stared Gary for a minute "So, you fucking called us here for nothing". Gary smiled. "I will fucking punch you in the face. Son of a bitch".

"Cool down man. There is a football tournament going on". "I don't wanna play" I cut in between. "So, let's go to my pool?" Gary said. "Nah, not now" I replied.

"So, we..." Gary thought, "We should go to the mall". "What... for shopping. Are you a girl? " Henry said.

"Then...".

"Stop... we are not going anywhere".

"Yes, we are. We can go to the girl's hostel".

"Bad Idea". "Totally bad idea" Henry said. "But we can go meet Naysa... Maria, Vanessa" I smiled. "Henry, you know Finn have a thing for Naysa"

"Really, Finn you didn't tell me about this" Henry placed his hand over my shoulder. "You are not good at reading minds and eyes, " I said. "Ouch... that was mean"

Naysa is the girl I've loved since the fourth grade. "Do you have any idea where she is?" Gary asked. "Probably she is at her home". "Okay, well, I'm driving," said Henry. "Really? Do you have any idea how to drive? Nah, I can't risk it, it is not a test car"

"Alright, I'm not driving. Why are you so mean today," Henry exclaimed. "We'll do a thing. First, I'll drive Finn to Naysa's, then Henry to Maria's, and then I'll pick up Vanessa".

"What the fuck dude... My car is not a truck" I raged. Gary stepped backwards "You are really mean today".

"Firstly, you called us here for nothing and you both are saying senseless things". "So, what to do now?" Henry asked. "We can take my car". "Your car is back?"

"Yeah... it is back". All right, but I'm going to drive your car. It has only 2 seats" I told Gary. "Are you sure? You cannot even talk to her, when we all are together". "Yes, I'm 100% fucking sure". "Any way you want man". We drove to Gary's and I gave my seat to Gary. I sat in Gary's car and drove it out of the garage. "Meet me at our sunset place" Gary said.

The car was running like a butter. *It's so smooth, I'll tell Gary to exchange it with mine.* I reached Naysa's house. I knocked at the door, but nobody responded. I knocked the door twice after that, still no one answered. No one's home, maybe she's out.

I moved back and was walking to the car "Hey... Finn". I turned around, it was Naysa. *Naysa, is she real. Goddamn it, she's beautiful. Her eyes... My god.* I got lost in my head. "Hey Finn... are you okay?" Naysa came close to me and laid her hand on my shoulder.

My mind boggled. "Yes... I'm more than fine now." I began to stutter. "Are you sure... Your face". "What about my face" I started rubbing my face. "Stop... it turned red. You are blushing". "Am I ? "

"Why were you not opening the door?". "I was listening to music upstairs, I wasn't sure if someone was at the door. Then I saw you going back to your car from the window". "Oh". *Her voice, It's so sweet. Don't stop. I can listen to you all day.*

"You are again silent. Are you not well or is it as always that you cannot speak in front of me?"

"No... What no... I'm talking". "I know that... you always ignored me when I tried to talk to you". "That is absolutely a wrong statement. I never ignored you".

"Didn't you? I noticed it all. Every-time, when we were having a conversation, you never spoke a word and you walked". *Then how come you haven't noticed I Love you. How can I explain this to you.* "You are just noticing things too much". "You just mocked me".

My body started sweating.

"Relax... I'm just kidding. But in fact, I've seen you speak to other girls freely. But you cannot do that with me. Can you? Am I different? Is something wrong with me?"

How can I explain you are special. Whenever I saw you my world just stops. I have butterflies in my stomach. Your voice, it's sweeter than honey. Your eyes, I just want to look in your eyes, but when you look back...

"Yes... you're right" Naysa sounds angry. "What... how? You can read minds?". "You have lost somewhere again; you must be thinking something. You were smiling". "Sorry... but Different? Yes, definitely you are different. Something wrong with you? No, there's not one thing about you that's not right. Every fucking thing is beautiful about you". *What... I just told her that. I can't fucking believe me.* "Really?" Naysa blushes "You are cute".

CHAPTER FOUR

ALL DAY, ALL NIGHT.

"How come you were here?". "I'm here for you!" Naysa lifted her eyebrows. "I want to say that I'm here to take you to the beach. All of us are going. Me, Gary, Henry, Maria & Vanessa".

"Whoa... nobody told me about it". "It has just been decided now. Gary is taking Maria & Vanessa".

"Okay, hold on one second, let me get my keys. I don't wanna stay outside".

We were sitting in the car and I was riding the car slow, not so slow. I don't normally drive slowly. "This car is so beautiful". "Yeah, it is... But this beauty is not mine. It's Gary's".

"So, What are we going to do at the beach?". "Not the beach, there's one place by the beach. We found that place. From there, the sunset is so beautiful".

"Wohoo... means you boys found that place?"

"Yes... usually no one comes there and there everything is silent. No peoples, no noice pollution, adding the view from that place just magnificent". "Amazing... now I'm excited".

This drive with you & your smiling face, I will never forget this. It would be so much more awesome if it was just, you and me.

We reached there. I saw my car parked. I parked next to mine. "They are here". "They have already arrived. We should go fast". I took her to our spot. We saw that everyone was sitting on a rock. Everyone was waving their hands towards us. We waved back.

"Walk carefully".

Naysa was sitting next to María and I was sitting next to Naysa. "Have you been here before?" Naysa asked Maria & Vanessa. "Never, But I'm glad they bring us here" Maria said.

"You were right, it's quiet here and it's beautiful" Naysa said. "Save your words, the sun has not even touched the water". We all were sitting in a line. After 10 minutes, the sun was about to set. "Now, see the beautiful setting-sun".

Everyone was watching the sunset. The sky was orange and yellowish. Suddenly, Naysa laid her head upon my shoulder. I was fucking astonished. All were staring at us.

What... This is a dream. She laid her head on my shoulder. What the fuck... My face was looking normal from outside, but inside my head my emotions, feelings, everything fucking goddam thing is bursting.

Gary was nodding his head with a weird smile on his face. "This is really overwhelming," Naysa said softly. "Told YA..."

After sundown, we returned to our car. "Hey man... after dropping her home I'll be at your place" I told Gary. "Sure bro".

We were driving back to Naysa's. "Today was great. Thanks to you" Naysa moved her hand on my hand. "By all means". *Should I tell her that I love her. Wouldn't it be too early. Early? God, I've been waiting since forever.*

"So, you are alone today? Your mom and dad aren't home?" I asked. "Yes, they have gone for some work and are coming after a week". "What do you say we go out to dinner?"

"You asking me out on a date?". "What..." My heart rate started to rise "No... No... just as a friend". "Relax... I'm teasing. I want to, But..." *This fucking but. The but word should not be fucking there.* "I'm going to my uncles for one week. They are picking me up at 8".

"That's cool". *It's really not.* I stopped the car as we reached Naysa's house "So this is it for today". "Yeah... it was nice hanging out with you" Naysa said, "So you want to say something?". "Me? No," I replied. *WTF... why did I answer so fast. Why is she even asking me this question. I hate myself.* "OK then..." Naysa stepped out of the car. "Bye..."

"Don't say bye. Say see you soon".

"See you soon..."

I reached at Gary's. They both were standing beside my car. I parked Gary's car in his garage. "Tell me... what was that?" Gary looks excited. "What was what?". "Head on your shoulder? What did you talk about?".

"Nothing bro... there is nothing that you think happened. Probably she still has no idea that I love her". "You should have told her about that" Henry said. "It is not that easy. But I'll tell her one day".

Then I dropped Henry off at his place and went back to my place. *Already missing her. Wish you were here with me all day, all night.*

Today is May Nineteenth. I'm bored sitting at home. "Hey guys... do you copy?" I used my walkie talkie.

"It's Gary. I copy. Over". "What are you doing bro? Over". "Thinking about going for a swim. What about you?

Over". "Nothing, just lying in the bed. Over". "Where is Henry? Henry, do you copy?".

"I'm bored at home". "I'm coming at your house to pick you. I have a work to complete. See you in 20. Over," said Gary.

After 30 minutes, he showed up and yelled my name out of his car. "Coming" I too yelled from my window.

"What is it? Where we headed to?". "My father forgot to pick up his papers with him. So, we are going to give him this" Gary showed his bag. "Where is Henry? He didn't even answer". "I don't know man". "Hold on a second, let me drive".

I sat on the driver seat and Gary on the passenger seat. "Where to?" I asked. "a couple blocks from our school". "Buckle up." I started driving. "I love your car; you can trade it with mine" I started driving faster. "Definitely not," Gary replied "Man, slow down".

"This is so smooth". "Dude... that's fucking fast" Gary shouted. We got there in the blink of an eye. "What the hell was that... what the fuck?" Gary freaked out. "Relax boy... where's your father?"

"We have to get into that building, it's there" Gary pointed his finger at a building. "Wohoo... it's fucking huge. Let's go".

We got inside the building. It was huge from inside. We got into an elevator. On the tenth floor, Gary's father's office was there. We gave him his document bag and left.

"Let's go check on Henry now". "Yes... no... You son of a bitch I'm driving now. Hand over the keys". "Why man..." Gary was driving.

We knocked at Henry's, but no one answered. "What do you think?" I asked Gary. "Maybe he is gone somewhere". "Whatever bro... drop me home. We'll ask him about it tomorrow".

At around 9 PM "Hello guys. Anyone copy? It's Henry" walkie spoke out of sudden. "Hey bro... its Finn. Where were you at? Over". "It's Gary. I copy. Over". "Last night, I have not slept. So, I slept all day and my mom shifts are from 3 to 8 now" after 30 seconds "Hello... you guys left?".

"You didn't say over. I thought you didn't finish yet," I replied. "Yes, you didn't say over". "All right... we were worried about you. See you tomorrow. Over" I said.

After three days. On May Twenty-second Me and my family was departing to Westerville to visit my grandmother.

Before I leave, I met those two idiots and told them not to end up missing or do something stupid without me, specially to Henry. I was going to meet them after 6-7 days now.

We reached Westerville; it is a small beautiful town I love to visit here to see my grandma.

On May Twenty sixth we heard from dad's friend that in our town it was raining. *Rain in summer...? It is quite abnormal.*

It's 1 AM of May Twenty-eighth and I am so tired. After a week of peregrinations, I finally reached our town, Stonington. I couldn't wait to meet Gary and Henry and tell them what I did at Westerville.

The next day, I tried to reach Gary and Henry through the walkie-talkie, but they didn't respond. So, I walk to Henry's house, but there was no one at home.

Henry and Gary were in the town garden. "Hey... I looked everywhere? Where are your talkies?" I asked, sitting with them on the swing. "We were just talking about you," Gary mummer. "All right... I am here".

Then I told them everything about Westerville and what I had done there and they heard everything. "Sounds like you had a lot of fun there," says Henry. "I did". "Were you missing us?" Gary asked. "Yes... I really missed you both"

"Did you know that it rained," said Gary. "What... yeah, I heard that it was raining in our town ere-yesterday"

"It's quite abnormal that it was raining in the month of May" Gary said while thinking something. "It was an abnormal rain" I said. "Besides, that day our professor Steve had met with an accident," Gary said. "What...? How? Is he alright?" I asked while alighting from the slide.

"He's not in danger now". "It's a relief," I said while observing that Henry was sitting quietly. "What's the matter with you? Why you are not saying anything" I asked Henry. "Nothing... It's about the accident" Henry replied.

CHAPTER FIVE

SPECIAL GUESTS.

"Did you dreamed anything after that day" I asked Henry. "Yes, I had a dream on May Twenty-third, but nothing happened." We both were addled. "Great... that one dream was just a coincidence".

"Are you still sleeping with that pillow?" Gary asked Henry. "No, I kept it in a box" Henry answered. "Did your grandfather gave you anything else?" I asked. "Yes, a scarab locket" Henry said. "What's a scarab?" Gary asked.

"It's a beetle shaped locket" Henry described. "Wohoo... that's cool" Gary said. "Are you carrying it with you at the moment?" I asked. "No, last time I checked, it was in the store room" Henry said.

It was getting dark. "Guys I forgot to tell you, we and some of our friends are going to Paradise resort".

"What... have you talked to your father?" I said "what about our friends?". Yes, I talked about it and all reservations are made and by friends, I mean Naysa, Maria, Vanessa & Jean" Gary murmured while standing from the swing. "We should go," Henry said. "We have to now, " Gary said.

"How and when are we going?" I inquired. "We all are going in a bus and we are leaving tomorrow morning, 10

AM" Gary said.

"What...??" Henry and I startled. "So far, my mother must have spoken with your mothers," Gary smiled. "Still, we have to pack our clothes and stuff" I blurted. "Yeah, we should go," Henry said. "All right, gather tomorrow in the garden at 10 AM sharp" Gary said.

After I got home, I packed all my stuff and clothes to wear and I wondered if I had left something to take away. *Everything's done... but what about the accident, dreams and nightmares. Let's not think about that and focus on the trip, I mean sleep.*

It's May Twenty-ninth. I reached the garden at 10AM and saw that Naysa had already arrived. "Hey... Good Morning" I said. *She is so pretty.* "Hey Finn... Good Morning" Naysa said, handshaking. "You're looking beautiful by the way" I told Naysa and she blushed.

"Are you excited for the trip?" She asked. "Yes, very much....". "Well, you must sit beside me in the bus." I said gladly. "Of-course, why not".

"Let's go, what are we waiting for?" I asked everybody. "That... we're waiting for that fatty running" Gary told pointing his finger towards Henry. "On time... On time..." Henry said while catching some breath.

About 4 girls were there out of which one was Naysa. So about we 7 people were going to Paradise resort. Naysa said she would sit next to me, although she didn't because of the girls.

Henry was sitting with Gary at the last seat and I was sitting ahead of them and the four girls were sitting in the front, side row. "When will we get there?" I asked Gary. "Around 5-6 PM" Gary answered. "OH, so I should sleep" Henry said. *Yes, for sure he is lazy, we just sat and he is sleeping.*

After 5 minutes of sleeping, Henry started snoring. "Do you have a clip?" I turned around. "No, why?" Gary looked at his bag. "His snore is ruining the mood". Gary and the girls laugh out loud "Really man, you are funny".

I decided to not focus on Henry's snore, then I caught sight of Naysa. She was talkin' to the girls. "Hey Girls... what are you talking about?". "Talking about you actually" Vanessa told me with a mysterious smile.

"Wohoo, what about me?". "Nothing, I was talking to them about the day you picked me up for sunset. It was so fun" Naysa clasped Vanessa's hand and made an eye gesture. "Yeah, it was...".

Did Naysa stoped Vanessa from saying something? I could tell that Naysa was saying something through her eyes to Vanessa. "Have you noticed anything, Finn?" Gary suddenly expressed himself. I turned around "What?".

"We've been sitting for an hour, the girls were gossiping whole time and they still are. They have so much to talk about" Gary said. "Yeah, that's for sure they have" I chuckled. "And see this our fatty is still sleeping. I'm bored".

"I'm bored as well. I thought it was going to be fun to travel together".

"Tell me about Naysa. Have you told her how you feel? " Gary mumbled. "No bro. I will. I never got a chance to say anything". "Come on, you did"

"Yeah, I will tell her on the trip". The bus stopped at the gas station. Gary and Henry had to pee. Maria and Jean went to the shop. "Are you bored?" Naysa asked me. "Nope, not that much" I run my hand over my hair.

"I'm also here guys, do your romance in private" Vanessa said. "Stop Vee, we are not doing anything" Naysa cried.

I was astounded, motionless. "Yeah, I saw that hair thing Finn did and you both were kept staring at each other". "No, we are not staring at each other".

I didn't say a word. I could tell Naysa's cheeks were turned pink. My face was still, so from inside a thousand butterflies were flying in my stomach. Then again, our eyes met.

We were back on our way. I just can't take my eyes off from Naysa. As I was staring, she suddenly looks back at me, but I turned my face. She saw. *Ugh, it was awkward.*

It's 2 PM. We stopped at a restaurant for our lunch. After lunch all were taking naps in the bus except me. *She is looking more beautiful while sleeping.*

My body was hurting from sitting for hours in the same seat. At Around 6:30-07:00 we reached the Paradise resort. The resort was small but was so beautiful. "We should go for trekking at night in the forest" Maria said. "Yeah... we definitely should" Gary said.

Everybody was so energetic when we got here. 3 rooms were booked, one for the boys and 2 for the girls. Everyone was talking about trekking, although everyone fell asleep after dinner.

It's 10 AM of May Thirty and It's a beautiful morning. Everyone was assembled in the main lobby. "Good morning my little fellows. My name is Patrick Christopher Richards" Patrick said.

Patrick owns the resort. He is a tall 40-45 years old. "I'd never guided any of my guests, for them, I've guides, as you all are our special guests, I'd love to do so, I assure you all, these 3-4 days will be the best of your life" Patrick said confidently.

Gary's dad made us special guests here. Patrick told us to gather around the pool after breakfast and take another pair of clothes with us. After having our breakfast, we gathered at pool side.

"How did you sleep last night?" I asked to Naysa. "I slept well, what about you". "Yeah, it was good".

"Hello My children, Today I'm going to show you the world's greatest waterfall and after that I'm going to take you to the zoo" Patrick told while showing some of the pictures of waterfalls and zoo.

"Zoo... we are not children" Jean said. "This is no ordinary zoo you will find surprising" Patrick assured. *He is using the word greatest in the world, let's see what is it.*

"Did you dream anything yesterday?" I asked Henry. "No... I slept peacefully yesterday" Henry said. "That's good, " Gary said.

We all were traveling to the waterfall Patrick was talking about, through bus. Along the way we saw different beautiful places and Patrick told us about them.

We had to pull the bus away from the waterfall that we have to walk to the waterfall. Everybody got off the bus.

"Listen, my children, I would walk in front of you all and Camille would walk in the back. Avoid touching sharp leaves or any leaves. Do not fall apart from the group or else you would be lost and there are no channels here. We may also find wild animals here, if any animal appeared there is no need to be panic. I will handle the situation".

Patrick was instructing us. "Can you hear that..." I told Naysa. "Yes, I can..." said Naysa. "What... I can't hear a thing" Henry and Vanessa said. "The waterfall..." Naysa said cheerfully closing her eyes.

We walked about half a mile; each step increases the noise from the cascade. "We reached... see there," said Patrick, pointing his finger at the waterfall "Isn't it beautiful?"

"The waterfall is as beautiful as you," I said to Naysa. Her cheeks turned pink. The water is falling from so high that it cannot be seen, it was more like the water is falling from the clouds and it was so beautiful.

"So, who wants to dance in the rain," stated Patrick. All except Jean were enjoying dancing in the waterfall. She cares about her makeup more, though she was enjoying seeing us. We enjoyed a lot; we had taken lots of pictures together.

After that, we changed our clothes in the bus, one after one. "Now we're heading to the zoo," said Patrick, lighting the bus engine. "But... we're hungry" I said, all agreed. "I know, we'll have our lunch in the restaurant by the zoo"

After lunch, we drove to the zoo. The zoo was looking amazing from outside. "Here boys and girls wear your batches and don't lose," Patrick said.

"I'm excited," said Naysa. "So am I," I said. Then after we all sat in a crazy shaped vehicle and in that vehicle, we have to travel the zoo. As the gates opened, a huge field is there. All the animals were freely moving here and there.

"I've never seen a lion and tiger from this close, " I said to all. "Me neither, " Henry said. "This is more of a forest than a zoo," said Naysa. "Yes, you are right, my child, it is only a forest," declared Patrick.

Patrick told different things about animals and about how they had been extinct in different part of the world. After that we walked into the underground aquarium.

"Magnificent... it's like a tunnel," Henry said as he walked into the aquarium. "See there, all the fish..." Gary told while clicking photos on his camera. Everything was so beautiful from within; sharks, fish and all aquatic animals were seen from within.

After traveling all day, we arrived at the resort at 7:00PM. "Did everybody enjoy today?" asked Patrick. "Yes, we enjoyed it a lot today," I said first and foremost. Then after everyone said that they enjoyed. "Today was only the beginning, you will all see places more beautiful than that," said Patrick.

"You can all sleep after having your dinner, dinner will be ready around 8 PM. Until then, you can all freshen up," says Camille. Camille is the lady working in the resort.

After cleaning ourselves, we all gathered in the hall. The smell coming from the dining table was so good. Then we all had our delicious dinner. After that, everyone was sitting with their legs in the pool. There wasn't a lot of water in the pool. Naysa was sitting by my side.

"Did you enjoy today?" I asked her. "Yes... today was incredible, I'm excited for tomorrow" Naysa responded. "Whatever it is, it would be fun".

"What is it about Vanessa? Is something wrong with her? She's been acting weird lately," I told Naysa. "No, she only likes to tease us by saying things like that". I blushed "I see". "Now we are close right?". "Now? We were! " I exclaimed. "No, we were not. Now you are talking to me without any hesitation. Unlike before".

"Stop saying that, till when you are going to say that". "Your entire life, it was like that. Huh".

"Do you want to be with me my entire life?" I smile. Naysa blushed "You're flirting". "You said yourself that".

Naysa again placed his head on my shoulder and again everyone was looking at us. *I think she loves putting her head on my shoulder.*

"You don't mind, do you?" Naysa said gently. "Not at all, I would never mind that. As a matter of fact, I love it and your smell is so sweet".

I'm way out of line. "Really? I don't think so". *Whoa man, her voice. It's also so sweet. Everything about her is so Sweet. She is a baby.* "I think... No, I mean your smell is so sweet". She didn't replies back.

"Naysa...". Is she asleep on my shoulder. She was sleepin'. I gently moved and laid her head on my lap. "Vee, can you get her legs out of the pool?". "Sure".

She gently takes her legs out of the pool. "Time to go to sleep. Come on, " Gary said. "Shh... she is sleeping. Drop your voice. You go, I'm coming".

"Okay, man. We are going to the room". "Yes, we all are too going. Tell her we are sleeping in our room as soon as she wakes up" Jean said.

You're looking more beautiful while sleeping. A lot more on my lap. I touched her cheeks. Her skin was as soft as cotton wool. *Fuck, your skin is so soft.*

I started playing with her hairs because of which she's awake. She sat "What are... did I fell asleep here". "Yes, well, sorry to wake you up".

"No... no, no, I'm sorry because of me you are still awake. You must be tired. Let's go back to our room" Naysa said Speedily. "Relax, no sorry".

Then the two of us went back to our rooms. I'm tired, but the thing that just happened was just fucking awesome.

CHAPTER SIX

TREKKING.

"Good morning..." Gary said. "Good morning, Gary. Henry is still sleeping". "Yes... he snored a lot last night," said Gary as he stared at Henry. "Should I get in the shower first?" I asked Gary. "Sure, I'll wake Henry up."

Then after we all showered consecutively and we called the girls to the dining room to have breakfast.

"Good morning... breakfast is ready" Camille said. We all had breakfast and then Patrick called us by the pool again today.

It's 9:30 AM of May Thirty-first. "Bonjour... today we're going to an island" Patrick said. This came as a surprise to all of us. "What a... an island," Henry said, taking photocopies of the island from Patrick. Patrick nodded.

"Are we staying there?" Jean asked. "Yes, we are staying there for 2 days and 1 night" Patrick replied. "It's amazing... it would be so much fun," said Naysa. "So, pack clothes of two days and some stuff that you want, we are leaving at 10 AM" Patrick said as he was taking a bite of the apple.

We all gathered at the main gate at 10 AM, the bus was ready to take us to the seashore. From the shore, motorboat would take us to the island. That's what Patrick talked about.

"Have a seat, children," said Patrick when he opened the bus door. "How far is the shore from here?" I asked Patrick. "The shoreline is only half an hour away," Patrick answered.

We all sat in the bus and we all were singing songs together. Though the sweetest voice was of Naysa.

On arriving, we saw that the boat was prepared. "Come on, kids, get in the boat one by one and have a seat," said Patrick as he took his driver's seat. "Are you driving?" wondered Vanessa.

"Indeed, you think I'm old for piloting a boat?" Patrick replied. "No, that's not it," said Vanessa while we were all laughing. We all sat down in the boat and after about a half hour we saw a little island.

"Can you all see that, the island" Naysa said pointing his finger. "Yes... it's so tiny from here," said Gary. "What is the name of the island?" I asked Patrick. "The island is called **W ISLAND**" he replied.

The island was looking beautiful from here. There were people on the beach of the island, enjoying. "So, there is another resort on the island that is yours?" Henry asked Patrick.

"Yes, my child, in-fact the whole island is mine. Only special guest is allowed here" Patrick replied and we all were shocked. "The whole island is yours" Jean asked. "Yes, my child, I own the island" Patrick replied smilingly. "What is the name of the resort?" Jean asked. "It's seashore resort."

We all reached there, we were all greeted by Patrick's assistant. Here we are, we have a separate room for everyone. "Today, you all get to do what you want on the island. You can enjoy at the beach side, you all can go for trekking, you all can ride the boats if you know how to swim. Just tell me before you do or go somewhere," Patrick said, showing us the small bedrooms.

We all were so excited to peregrinate the whole island. We all put our bags and stuff in our rooms. We all gathered under a big palm tree near the beach. We were deciding what to do.

It was around 11:30 AM. "What are you thinking about doing...? Should we go for trekking?" I asked Naysa. "We can do that...," said Naysa.

After half an hour I, Gary and Naysa decided to go for trekking in the forest. We all goes to meet Patrick. He told us about other activities too. Henry and Jean decided to go for rafting in the evening with other peoples.

"We three decided to go for trekking" I said while pointing fingers at Gary and Naysa. "That's great... but convince 2-3 more, so I can organize a trekking competition," said Patrick. "A trekking competition... that sounds great" Naysa said.

Then we told Henry, Jean, Maria & Vanessa about the competition. "A trekking competition. I will join you," Maria said as she rose from the chair. "Me too..." Vanessa agreed with Maria. "Henry...? Jean? You would like to join us?" Gary asked. "I don't like trekking," Henry said with his hat on. "Well, let's talk to Patrick about it," I said.

We told Patrick María and Vanessa would be joining us. He told us that he will meet us at the front gate from where the forest starts in about half an hour as he wants to arrange everything for the competition. After half an hour, we all gathered at the forest gate. Patrick was there as well, speaking with their staff.

"Are you all ready... there are no rules, the first one to finish will win and the winner will get a trophy with a cap and T-shirt of the resort. Firstly, you have to walk in the forest which would take about an hour and a half and then you have to go through the giant trees, you have to find your way out of the giant trees. Then you have to cross the river by means of a little boat on your own. This are the 3 Levels and it's easy. 4ᵗʰ & 5ᵗʰ levels are difficult. You can even end up lost in the forest. Though no need to worry, there are my people all around the forest and". As Patrick was saying, Gary interrupted and said, "Is there anyone who can guide us?". "No external help, they will not help you in guiding ways" Patrick said.

"There are also green buttons at each checkpoint, if you want to stop or if you're lost, you can press the button. In the fourth level, you must climb a small mountain, my people will be there to assist you and see that you are all safe. In the final level, you all have to go through a huge maze. People end up quitting in the last level. But there are hidden clues everywhere, if you see clearly, you can find a way forward" Patrick said with a map in his hand.

There Patrick gave us trekking clothes and we all changed our clothes in the changing room along with it, he also gave us a bag and some things were there in the bag.

"If you're hungry, there's milk, chocolate drinks, fruits, and chips in your bag. In the bag you will also find a watch, a map and a compass. Take it out, wear the watch and put the compass in your pocket" Patrick said while taking a whistle from one of his staff members.

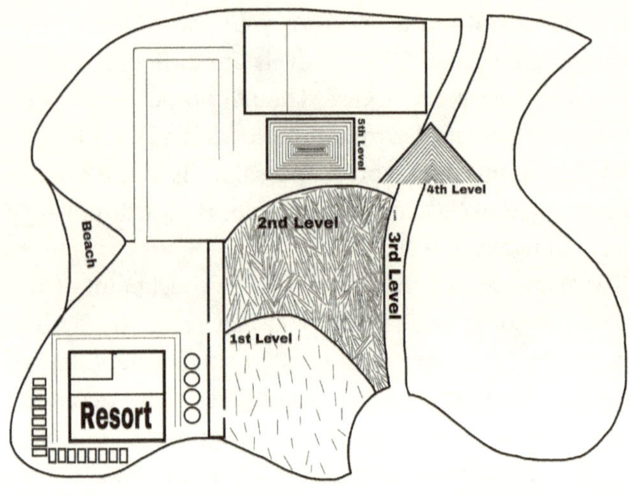

W ISLAND

"Compass...". Before I could say anything Patrick cut-in between and said "In the first two levels you must go straight north and after third level you must go west till the last level. Are you all ready for it?" "Yes, we are, it's challenging" Naysa replied. We all agreed with her.

Patrick opened the forest gate and said "There is no wild animal in the forest so no need to worry about it and the last thing, after you solve the maze, you will find cycles. There will be a number of cycles. You have to pick one and must ride to the entrance of the resort by cycling" Patrick said.

"We still have to get here through the cycle, all of it will take so long," Maria said. "Yes, it will take more than 5-6 hours or more until 7 sunlight will be there. It's almost 1 PM now. So, you all are ready?" Patrick asked, taking his whistle in his hand.

We all said we are ready then he wheezed and we all entered the forest and the gates were closed.

Upon entering, I said to Naysa, "I'm going to win...". "Let's see that, who's going to win," said Naysa. There were trees all around, we all separated on our own path. I took out the map and saw direction on the compass. While walking, I saw a hidden arrow showing where to go, in one of the trees.

I walked about an hour and a half in the direction indicated by the arrow, but I could not find the way out of level 1. After 10 minutes, I saw a gigantic tree. I ran to that tree and saw a board that wrote level two. I was glad to see the level two board. I looked around to see if there was anyone who finished level one, but there was no one there.

After half an hour of walking around the giant trees, I decided to take a 10-minute break because I was hungry and walking all the time. I sat for 10 minutes and I drank some milk and ate an apple. While again walking for 10 minutes, I heard the sound of the water and I immediately ran towards it.

I saw Maria at the other end of the river. There were two boats on the other side which means two people are ahead of me. I took a boat and swing my arms with oars in the water as fast as I could.

The boat was shaking right and left in the water, but somehow, I reached the other side and while getting off from the boat I step my one leg in the river by mistake.

There were green color buttons everywhere. Having crossed the river, I saw the mountain, Naysa and Maria was climbing the mountain. The resort staff gave me a helmet and a glove. They also helped me tie the carabiner with a string so that if I fall nothing happens to me.

The mountain was small, I climbed the mountain in 10 minutes and I saw a roller coaster. There was an amusement park on the island, which is clearly visible from the top of the mountain. It took me another 5-10 minutes to descend the mountain.

Maria was still climbing the mountain, but Naysa was not there. Naysa is surprisingly good; she is first and in the last level. I saw a board and on it was written **Jungle Maze-The last level**. I walked into the maze with no idea where to go. The map and compass weren't as helpful.

I found it very confusing. I think, it keeps on going, it doesn't end. I kept coming back to this place over and over again. I was walking inside the maze for about an hour. I sat on the floor; I was tired walking here and there. I drank the chocolate drink. I sat for 10 minutes.

There are many marked arrows in this maze. I think the purpose of these arrows is to create confusion. I was continuously walking left-right-left-right.

I stopped in an area where the color of the leaves is slightly different. I saw a clue behind a leaf, there was **SEVEN STEPS L-R-L-L-R-L-L-R**. At first, I was not able to identify what was written, then I acknowledge that L for left and R for right.

I was certain it would help me win. I memorized the steps, then I did exactly what this note said. When I got there, there was also the color of the leaves were different. I started looking for another piece of hint. I took right, but nothing was there. I got back in that area, then I turned left and the exit was there.

"Whoa... I did it. I fucking did it," I shouted.

CHAPTER SEVEN

HIDE & SEEK.

I ran towards the exit, there were cycles and behind that, there was a huge gate of a park named Funville. I took a cycle on the road and paddle it as fast as I can.

I was on the way to the entrance of the resort and I saw Naysa ahead of me. I paddled as fast as I could. I passed Naysa.

Then I realized that she deserves to win, She was ahead of everyone. I slowed my speed and let Naysa pass me so that she could win.

Patrick with some other peoples were standing there and Naysa reached the entrance before me. We both got off from the cycle. "Congratulations... you won" Patrick told Naysa. "You won" I said while doing handshake. "Told YA... I would win."

"Let's gets inside..." said Patrick. As we enter the resort, Gary, María and Vanessa were already there. We both were surprised. "You all quit...?" I asked. "I was lost in the first level only, Vanessa quit in the 2nd level and Maria in the maze. Only you two finished the contest," Gary said while sitting on a chair.

"May I have your attention; The winner of the competition is Ms. Naysa. Here you go..." Patrick said, handing a small trophy, a T-shirt, and a cap to Naysa. All of us clapped. I was happy that she won.

"It's 6:30 PM, you all can rest now. Dinner will be served at 8:00-8:30 PM. Thank You all..." Patrick said.

Then we all returned to our rooms. I slept for approximately 2 hours. At 8:30, Gary knocked and told me to come at the dinning place. I washed my face and left; everybody was seated. I sat alongside Henry.

"What was it like today...? How did it go?" I asked Henry. "It was so much fun... we went for river rafting and, in the evening, Patrick took us in the middle of the ocean" Henry replied. "Sounds fun...".

After our lovely dinner, we went straight to the beach. We all were sitting on the deck chair. "Have you seen that park by the maze?" I asked Naysa. "Yes, the Funville park... I saw its entrance" Naysa replied drinking orange juice.

Then Patrick came and told us to follow him. He was walking to the right side of the beach. "We saw a park in front of the maze... is it closed?" I asked Patrick while walking. "No, it's not closed, I'll come back to it later." He answered.

We saw some people dancing to loud music and there, assorted colors lights were scattering all around. "You all have to dance now; the party is started" Patrick said. "Let's dance..." Gary said. All of us danced for half an hour and then decided to play hide and seek.

It was Gary's turn to seek, we all were hiding. Naysa was hiding with me. Near beach side there were huge rocks. We were hiding behind one a huge rock near the beach side.

"Gary could never find us here, " I said while Naysa was starring me. "Why did you do that?" Naysa asked. "What..."

I asked ambiguously. "Why did you slow down your bicycle?" she cried out loud.

"Shh... Gary could find us if you speak this loudly" I said gruffly. "Then tell me..." before she could say anything, I clamped my hand over her mouth. "Yes, I deliberately slowed down so that you might win."

"Why did you want me to win?" She goes on asking. "I don't know... I just want you to win because you deserve to win" I replied. No, that's the wrong answer, whoever is one step ahead of everyone deserves to win. You crossed my path and slowed your bicycle".

I was sweating because of Naysa's questions. "Are you going to tell me or not?" She again yelled.

"Because I LOVE YOU" I said unconsciously. I realized after I said that. *What, did I said I LOVE YOU.* "I'm sorry... I wasn't going to say that," I said. "Did you mean it?" she wondered. "What... yes, I mean that," I answered looking down. "I want to hear that only...". "What...? Why...? " I asked.

Am I supposed to ask her if she loves me or not?

"I want to give you something, like you helped me win the contest," she said, and then suddenly Gary showed up. "Found you..." He screamed.

Wow... What a fucking wrong timing, Naysa was going to give me something. Son of a bitch. "I found all" Gary exclaimed. It was about 11:30 PM and we all decided to go and sleep.

"Meet me at the beach at 1 PM when all were asleep" Naysa whispered in my ear. I was in wonder like '*Why is she calling at 1? What is she going to give me*'. Though I had told her that I love her.

Should I sleep or not, I should wait. I feel kind of free now, Like I told the thing I'm hiding.

I waited an hour and it was 12:40, so I decided to hit the beach. I sat on the sand; the sea waves were larger and the full moon was brighter. I saw Naysa coming at around 12:50 AM.

"You are early, when did you come?" asked Naysa, while she was seated next to me. "I came around 12:40, you're also 10 minutes early" I answered. "Well... I was just thinkin' of you only," said Naysa. "About me... What?" I asked as she laid her face on my shoulder.

She adores putting her head on my shoulder. I lay my arm around her shoulder.

"It doesn't matter..." said Naysa. *You have a sweet voice and you smell really good.* "You wanted to give me something, right? What is it... you can give me, " I said.

She looked up and asked me to look in her eyes. I was scared. *You have a fucking beautiful eyes.* All of a sudden, she kissed me on the lips. *What just happened.* We both didn't speak a word for 2 minutes. "That's... that's what I wanted to give you" Naysa said blushing.

I can't believe she kissed me, I'm the luckiest person on earth. No, in the universe. I was confused, shocked.

"I'm amazed, it's like a dream to me" I said. "It's real, it's not a dream, " she said while again laying her head on my shoulder.

"Look today is a full moon night, " I said, but she didn't respond. "Are you asleep?" *She is again sleeping on my shoulder and she kissed me. This is all a miracle. Although I don't believe in magic, but it's a goddamn miracle. She again slept on my shoulder. She really loves that. I can sense your heart beating.* Then for an hour, I didn't move a muscle. Though I was sleepy, but I didn't want to wake her up.

CHAPTER EIGHT

IN THE MIDDLE OF THE OCEAN.

She moved her hand and then lift her head. "What time is it..." Naysa asked. I saw the watch and said "3:30 in the morning". "What? Were you awake all along?". "Yes... I was awake... I didn't want to break your sleep" I replied.

"Again... you do not have to do everything for me. This is the second time today. Now we should go and sleep in our rooms". "I love to see you sleep, feel your heartbeat". "Huh... Idiot" we both laughed.

We went back to our rooms. In the morning I woke up at 9 AM. Today is First of June of 1969. I quickly showered and then I knocked Gary's and Henry's door. They both were ready. "Did you call the girls?" Gary asked. "No, I haven't" I replied.

"You guys go ahead, I'll call the girls" I said. "Alright, we are going to have breakfast" Gary said while yawing. Then I knocked Naysa's door and she opened the door. "Are you ready? We're waiting" I asked. "I'm ready... wait here, I'll come in a bit, " She replied while going in the room.

Then I knocked Maria, Vanessa, and Jean's door. They all were also ready. Then Naysa came and we all were walking to have our breakfast. We saw Henry and Gary eating sandwiches.

As we sat on the table, Patrick came and said "Do not eat too much, Today we are going to the park". "By park, you mean Funville park?" I asked.

"Yes my child, the Funville park. So eat, but only a little bit. Once you all had your breakfast, gather at the entrance of the resort" Patrick replied.

Then we ate our breakfast and we all were walking towards the entrance gate. There was a bus ready and Patrick was speaking to some of their personnel.

It was almost 10 AM. "We all are leaving in 10mins, you all go and take your seats" Patrick said while he was placing some stuff in the bus. Then we all sat in the bus. I noticed that Henry was sitting silently and he hadn't said a word since the morning.

"What's the matter with you? Why are you so quiet?" Gary asked Henry. "Yes... what happened, do you want eat more," I said in jest, but no one laughed.

"No—Nothing, I'm just thinking about the park. It would be fun" Henry spoke after a while. "Are you sure about that...? Your face is saying something else" I interrogate. "What? I'm all good" Henry responded.

After 10 minutes Patrick came and started the bus "We'll reach in just 5mins". By the road the park was quite close, but by the forest it would take 4-5 hours to reach there. Although we were going to the park, I was wondering about last night.

"I want to say something to you..." I muttered so that only Gary and Henry could hear. "What?" Gary asked. "Last night my dream came true..." I replied. "What? How? Did something happen?" Henry questioned spontaneously. Henry seemed a little scared. "Calm down... I said a dream, not a nightmare". "What is it?". "Yesterday Naysa kissed me" I revealed.

"Hurray... Finally" Gary expressed. "Quiet, son of a bitch" I mumbled, Everyone was looking at us. "What happened Gary? You are looking so happy?" Jean asked. "Nothing... it's nothing".

"But when? Are you with us the whole time?". "When we were going..." as I was saying the bus stopped and Patrick bawled "We reached". "I will tell you later" I whispered. Then we all got off of the bus.

"What about the last night... My mind is kept on thinking about that only" I told Naysa while walking towards the main building of the park. "So do I. don't tell anybody" Like Naysa said I was lost in my thoughts that I had already told Henry and Gary about it. Maybe she doesn't want anyone to know about it.

"Don't worry... I won't tell anyone about it" I humbled. Patrick called and got us some clothes. We all switched clothes and went into the park. There were people in the park. "There is lots of rides in the park. You all can go on whichever ride you want, But as per the instructions of the ride" Patrick described.

There were rides throughout the park. Some of them were so huge. I was never been to an amusement park before. "Here... wear your batches and try not to lose it" Patrick gave the batches to all. We all wore the batches.

"Now you all can go enjoy the ride, the lunch time will be at 1 PM and the park closes at 6" Patrick said joyfully. We begin to see the rides in the park. "You have to be with me all the time" I told Naysa. "I'm with you only...".

There were too may rides, we were confused. We all decided to go the bumper car ride, then we took the ticket. We all sat and we have to ride our own vehicle and crash it into others. It was a fun ride.

After getting out from that ride, we decided to go for the roller-coaster. Henry was scared of all these types of rides, so he didn't join us.

"This is looking scary" I told Naysa. She sat right beside me. As then it begins at normal speed, at first the roller coaster was moving upwards slowly and suddenly it went downwards so speedily. Initially I closed my eyes, but then I felt incredible. The speed of the roller coaster was velocious.

"Where are we going now?" asked Maria, with one hand over Jean's shoulder. "We should now go to the drop tower." said Naysa. Then I, Naysa and Jean went to the drop tower and the rest went somewhere else.

After going to 2-3 more rides, it was almost 1 PM. All the rides were shut down until the end of lunch. We all then met at the place where the lunch was being served.

We all ate our lunch and we decided to rest for 20-30 minutes. We all sat under a shade of a tree. "Are you enjoying?" Naysa asked. "Yes... all the rides are amazing here." I replied.

"We should now go to **THE HAUNTED MANSION**" I said as everyone was confused about it. Gary and Jean agreed with me. After resting for 20 minutes, we took the tickets of the haunted mansion.

We stepped inside the mansion. It was kind of dark. No one can see anything in it. All of a sudden, a dummy came out of a window and scared us. Then we saw stairs, we climbed up, while climbing another big dummy came out of nowhere.

After 20 minutes, we all made it out of the mansion. "It was quite scary... the ghost was appearing out of sudden from everywhere" said Gary while catching some breath. It was almost 2:30 PM.

Naysa and I decided to go for the space travel. It shows us about how does the space looks like, what is in the space and everything else about the space.

Then we sat in some other rides and then we all were tired and we sat on almost every ride except the rides of the children. "It's 5:30 PM, the park will be closed at 6 PM. We should now go meet Patrick" Maria said while drinking water. All the rides in the park were so amazing.

We walked to the main building to meet Patrick. "You all are here, did you all enjoy?" Patrick asked as we all showed up one after one. We all said it was a great experience and we enjoyed a lot. "So, let's go back to the old resort" Patrick said.

All of us were confused. "To the old means...?" Jean asked. "To the old means, to the Paradise resort" Patrick replied. "Are we going there today?" I questioned.

"Yes my child, tomorrow is your last day and you all are leaving at night, so we must move back to Paradise resort. Before that you all can eat something at the Sea-shore resort and we'll have our dinner at Paradise resort" Patrick replied with a smile on his face.

Then we reached the resort of the island. We all were mournful that we have to leave this island. We packed our stuff took our bags and went to the eat something.

It was almost 6:30. After eating, We all sat in the boat and Patrick was ready on his driver seat. "We shall go now or else it would be dark, once the sun-set" Patrick said while starting the boat. All the staff members were there and when we were leaving, they were waving their hands at us.

The sun was setting and it was looking beautiful. We were on our way to shore, but all of a sudden, the boat stopped.

"Is everything all right...?" Naysa asked Patrick, as we were all afraid that the boat is stopped in the middle of the ocean. "Let me check" Patrick replied. "What's the matter?" I asked Patrick. "The motor of the boat is exhausted".

"What? How can we fill it?" Gary asked. "We need a new one, but we are in the middle of the ocean. "You don't have an extra motor? What can we do now" Vanessa asked. "How can this happen?" Naysa asked. "Why didn't you check it?" Jean asked.

We all hurled lots of questions to Patrick. "I'm so sorry for all this" Patrick anguished "This is all my fault". We all started to terrify.

"What will happen now? We all gonna die here" Vanessa startled. "Don't panic, my people will come looking for us" Patrick gave us assurance. But it's clear from Patrick's face that he's anxious.

Henry started crying. "Don't cry my child, stay calm. I will never let anything happen to you" Patrick promised. Everyone told Henry not to cry. Within about ten minutes, the sunlight was gone and everything was dark.

"Has one of you got a flashlight in your bag? Turn on your flashlight and you have walkie-talkie, right? see whether there is a channel available here or not" Patrick stated. "I have a torch" I took out the torch and switch it on.

We've all switched on our walkie-talkie and checked all channels. No one was there on any of it.

We all waited an hour, but nobody came looking for us. "Are you guys hungry?" said Patrick. We all said no as we ate some food before leaving.

"I don't think anybody's coming, we're trapped here" Gary expelled. "Everyone can survive till tomorrow. If no one came till tomorrow's morning, I will swim to the beach and then come to take you all" said Patrick dolefully "By chance any of you have some food in your bag?"

Jean got two packets of crisps, Naysa got an apple, Gary got two cans of cold drinks and I got a bottle of water. "That's all we have..." Naysa notify.

"Well, share and eat. You hadn't eaten in three hours," said Patrick. We all eat one packet of chips with Patrick. We cut the apple into 8 parts with Gary's cutter and gave one to each and drank a sip of water.

Still our tummy was not full, we decided to eat the other packet afterwards. "It's 10PM, you all should sleep" Patrick said. "Are you fine? Are you hungry?" I asked Naysa. "I'm good, are you alright?". "Yes, I'm fine."

It was so scary to be on the boat in the middle of the ocean and everything was dark. No-one can see anything in the dark.

At midnight, we had another package of chips and drank the cold drinks. After that I saw Naysa sleeping and fall asleep seeing her. I woke up at 7:00 in the morning, and I noticed Henry was awake. Henry didn't appears to have fallen asleep last night. His eyes were red. "Do you feel well? Have you been up all night?" I'm questioning him. "No... I didn't want to sleep, but now I'm hungry..." Henry quavered.

CHAPTER NINE

PERMISSION.

It was 7 in the morning; all were sleeping except me and Henry. From afar, I saw a boat coming toward us. I wake Patrick. He called out "Help... Help..." waving both hands "Help... Help...". When the boat approached, Camille was there.

Everyone was awake listening to Patrick's voice. "It's Camille, she's here to help us," Gary exclaimed. "Thank god..." Patrick ease. She adjoins the boat with our boat. "What went wrong?" asked Camille to Patrick. "The engine was exhausted and I noticed that the fuel was also finished". "You didn't show up yesterday, so I thought you were bringing the children today. But when I talked to Sophie, she said everyone had gone last night. So, I came" Camille explained. "Thank You, you came" Naysa thanked.

"Come on now transfer to that boat one by one" Patrick said. We all sat on Camille's boat and took off. "But how were you speaking to Sophie? There are no channels here" Gary asked. "I talked through pigeons..." Camille said piloting the boat. "What?" We were all astounded. "Yeah, we gave the letter to pigeon to deliver the message" Patrick said.

"What about that boat..." I asked Patrick. "I'll deal with it and I'm sorry about yesterday... it was my mistake" Patrick apologizes. "We can understand..." Naysa said.

Then we all reached the shore and sat on the bus. "Is everything all right, Henry? Are you hungry? I wondered; Henry was barely talking. "Yes, I am."

"Just few minutes my child, then you all can eat as much as you want" Patrick told Henry while driving the bus. We reached the resort after 10 minutes and we were so hungry that we all clashed on food and filled our tummy.

"I apologize for my mistake, my children; yesterday you all suffered because of me. None of that would have happened if I had checked the boat properly" Patrick express regret. "Forget about it, nothing happened to anyone. Everybody's fine now," said Naysa, and we all agreed with her.

"Although this has happened and is your last day here, do you all want to go somewhere or you all want to rest?" Patrick asked us. "I want to get some sleep," said Gary. I also said that I want to rest. Everyone said that they want to rest except Henry. He hasn't said a thing. It was clear looking to his face that he needs a good sleep.

I slept for about 3-4 hours and it was 1 in the afternoon. Gary and Henry were still sleeping. I did not disturb them and left the room. I saw Naysa going to the pool side, I followed her.

Naysa, Maria, Vanessa and Jean were having fun in the pool. "You're awake. Come join us," said Naysa, sipping orange juice. I dived into the pool. I pulled my T-shirt off and all the girls were looking at me. Naysa was angry at me the way she looked at me.

Naysa made a gesture through her eyes. Though I couldn't figure out what she was talking about. Then she makes the gesture again with her angry face. She's trying to tell me to put my T-shirt back on. I wore my t-shirt and then Naysa came close and said "You better should not do anything like this again. You got that?".

I had no idea what to say, so I shook my head. Gary and Henry came looking for us. Henry was looking better now. "You two are awake. Come..." as I was saying, Patrick abruptly came and said "The lunch is ready, be there in 10 minutes". Then we took a shower and left for lunch.

"Today is boring, there is nothing to do" Vanessa said. All of us were sitting in the main hallway. "We should ask Patrick if there's anything we can do here" Naysa said "He would tell us". "Yes, we should go and ask Patrick" I concurred.

Then we all were finding Patrick in the resort, but he was vanished. We found Camille and asked her about things to do here. "Sorry to say, but we cancelled all your plans and bookings for today, but there is a sport area at the back of the resort, you can ride bicycles, there is basketball court and football court you all can play there" Camille replied.

"Is it possible to explore the forest zone at the back of the resort?" asked Naysa. "You can, but you need to get Patrick's permission for that and he's not at the resort. He has some work to finish, he will be joining us in the evening. Which means you cannot go anywhere".

Naysa seemed unhappy. "But we will not do anything dangerous. We will just walk and come" I told Camille. "No, I won't give you any permission. If anything happens, I'm to blame. If you're interested in exploring, explore the resort. Although the resort seems small, it is large. I'll be in the main lobby, if you'd like something".

We all headed towards the theater to see if anyone was there or not. While walking to the theater, I pulled Naysa back and said, "Meet me in front of your room. I'll speak to Gary. Do not ask anything. Just do as I say, in 10 minutes". We looked inside the theater, nobody was there. "There is no one in the theater, if you want to watch a film, I can help you with it" Louis said. He was also one of the members of the resort. We told him to play any movie, so that our time just passed by. "I'm going with Naysa outside, alone. So, tell everyone to not follow us" I muttered in Gary's ear. "What? You are not watching?". "No...". The I left the theater and watching me Naysa also came.

"What are we going to do?" Naysa asked. "First, We're going to take a water bottle and then we're going into the forest". "What? But Camille didn't allow us to be there".

"Don't worry... We will go on the quiet".

Then we took a water bottle with us and sneakingly entered into the forest. "We will go straight from here and will come on the same path back, so we would not end up lost" Naysa said. "As you say...".

On the way, Naysa holds my hand. "What if Camille finds out we're here?" Naysa asked. "No one will find out. Let's just enjoy our last day".

After walking for nearly 20 minutes "Can you hear the noise from the water?" Naysa asked. "I guess it's the river". We rushed to the sound. There was a beautiful small river.

"It's beautiful. We should have brought everyone," said Naysa. "Nah... It feels good alone with you". "Really?". "Absolutely".

We splashed water on our face and sat along the edge of the river. "Patrick should have mentioned this beautiful place," I told Naysa.

We both were staring at each other. I pulled Naysa from the back and she sat on top of me. We started kissing each other. I was able to sense her breath. "Wow... it was unbelievable," I said. "Really? Am I kissing right?". "You are a Fucking awesome kisser".

"You haven't been out with anybody, have you?" asked Naysa. "Nope... never". Naysa smiled. "Now... let's head back to the resort before someone finds out we're here".

After 30 minutes we manage to reach the resort. All were in their room. "Let's get ourselves clean. Our clothes are dirty. Meet me in 20-30 minutes" I told Naysa.

"Where have you been? What were you both doing?" Gary asked me. "We were in the forest and we found a river it was lovely". "Really..." Henry expressed. "You son of a bitch. You told me you are going outside, but didn't say that outside the resort" Gary cried. "Next time..." I laughed at Gary.

"When are we leaving?" Henry asked Gary. "At around 9 PM, after dinner" Gary replied "You missing Home?". "Yes, I'm missing my home". It was still 5:30 PM. We all packed our bags. We somehow passed our time, by doing nothing. It was time to eat our final dinner at the resort. We ate our delicious lunch and then we all picked up our luggage and gathered at the entrance.

We all were placing our bags inside the bus. Patrick and his crew were standing. "I guess you all enjoyed at our resort, except that incident happened and I apologize for that mistake I made" Patrick said "You all are so sweet, and we gonna miss you all. Come back again soon". Then Camille gave us a bottle that said Paradise resort.

We thanked everyone and sat on the bus and were on our way back to our town. "It was so much fun here; I'm going to miss it" Naysa said. "Yea... we all gonna miss it" I said. "We would be at home till tomorrow morning, so we should sleep now" Gary said. After that, we all slept.

CHAPTER TEN

HOME SWEET HOME...

In the morning, at about 6:00, the driver uncle woke us all as we reached our town. All of us were still sleepy. We still had to walk to our homes out of the garden.

"Home Sweet Home... I'll catch up with you all later..." I told everybody. I knocked on the door of my house, but nobody responded. But I know where my mother stashes the key to our house under the flower plot.

I took the keys and opened the door and quietly moved to my room. I was still tired, so I put the bag and slept again. At around 11 AM, I woke up. Today is Third of June. I took a shower and went to check on my parents. Dad was at work, though.

"You're here... are you allright? I heard about what happened on the island" My mom said, seeing me carefully from top to bottom. "I'm alright... it was a great experience. We all had such a great time," I answered. "That's great... I missed you," she hugged me. "I missed you both so much".

I met my dad at night, he was also so happy that I'm back from my trip. Holidays are tedious to do nothing at home.

On June Forth, everyone was gathered in the school. Today is the announcement of our result. Naysa and Henry were with me. "Where is Gary?" inquired Henry. "I don't know man. He said he was going to join us, but he didn't".

"Good morning my lovely fellows...." One of the teachers is started giving some speech. One after one every teacher is giving some life lesson speech, still didn't get what they wanted to convey. They began to announce the names of students who passed and call us on the stage to give us a certificate and the result paper.

After an hour Me, Gary, Henry, Naysa, Maria, Vanessa & Jean were sitting in a class. "Congratulations guys... we all pulled it off. Let's celebrate" Gary was exhilarated. "Yes, let's do it...".

While walking through the hallway "Hey Finn... what are you doing today? Are you free?" Stacy asked. "No, he is not... Come on Finn, let's go" Naysa fumed. "Wait... what was that?" I asked Naysa. "What... nothing. Let's go they are waiting for us".

"Are you angry?".

"No, I'm not... she likes you and you know that". "Yeah... but I don't like her". "So why are you talking to her...?".

"I haven't said a thing. She was just asking me".

Naysa started walking faster "I know how they all stare you... I don't like that". "Hang on, slow down. There's nothing I can do if they're staring me". "I'm not coming... you all go" Naysa walked out of the school.

"Wait...." I screamed. "You all go... We will join you" I told everyone. All were staring at us and I was smiling at them.

I ran to Naysa and stopped her. "You are not angry with me, right? Now the high school is over, They will never meet us. Don't be angry with me. Please," I delightfully said. "No need to apologize. I'm not mad". "Now smile...".

She smiled. Seeing her smile, I automatically smiled "That's my girl". "Who told you I'm your girl?". "No one". "Then why do you call me your girl". "Because you are my pretty girl". Naysa blushed.

"Now, should we join them or go on our own somewhere else?" I asked. "For now, we should join them. We will go some other day". "As you say..."

On Fifth June, I was sitting with Henry at his house talking about college and other things. We were waiting for Gary. I noticed one thing that after that incident happened at the resort, Henry was more quiet. He didn't talk much, don't say anything, and as far as I know, he's very talkative. After 10 minutes, Gary showed up.

"I'm bored... we should do something or go somewhere" Gary cried. "What or where?" I asked.

"Let's plan something...". "Naysa is meeting me on seventh. I will talk to her about it".

Then we talked for an hour and drove off.

It's 1 PM of June sixth, Gary and Henry were sitting with me in the park. Again, today I saw Henry is sitting completely quiet. He was in some deep thoughts. "What's gotten into you...?" I asked. "No nothing...". "You always say that--tell us, what is it? Are you worried about anything? Did something happen" I demand.

"Today, I saw a cat died" Henry said. "You're quiet for that reason" Gary said "cats can only live for 15-20 years". "Don't think about that now, who did this cat belong to?" I asked. "I don't know and I'm not upset about it. I **DREAMED IT**" Henry screeched.

"What...?" I was shocked, "What are you talking about?". "Again..." Gary said. "It's been happening since the summer holidays started," Henry said. "What? I can't believe" I startled "First the dog, now cat? This are the only two things that happened, right?".

"No... everything happened because of my dream" Henry cried. "What do you mean by everything?" I asked. He started crying. "Can you speak... what do you mean by everything...?" I asked again. "You want to hear... so listen, first the dog chased me. Then I was trapped inside Gary's house, I dreamt it. I fell in my house, I dreamed it. Even the rain and the accident that happened to our teacher. We're even stuck in the middle of the ocean because of me and now that cat is dead because of me... I dreamed it all".

What's he talking about... Is it true...? If that's true, we all have serious problems. "Did you dreamed it all" I asked "Means you dreamed it before it happens". *What I'm asking.* "Yes, I dreamed what is going to happen tomorrow, but Only once in a week" Henry said. "What? Once a week?" wondered Gary. "Only one dream happened in real life in a week".

The whole thing was highly unrealistic. "It's Nightmares, not dreams" I apprised "Dreams are good, Nightmares means something bad". "Henry is dreaming Magical Nightmares" Gary spoke "Do you know what to do now?". "I have no idea what to do". "Why didn't you talk about this earlier" I asked Henry. "Because you were not believing me that day. You were telling it's just coincidence, its fate. If I had told you, you would still not believe me."

"I believe you now. You said that you also have a bettle shape pendant that your grandfather had given you" I told Henry. "Yes, I still have it, it's in the storeroom"

"Is your mother going to be there?" said Gary. "No, perhaps she's at work now, it's 3:00". "We should go find that pendant" I said. "Why? There's nothing about that pendant. It's just like the pillow" Henry said. "Though we should just see that pendant or you should wear that" I said.

Then we went to Henry's house. There was no one home. We walked to the store room. "When I saw, it was in a small box" Henry said. We all were finding a small box.

After 10 minutes of finding, Gary found a small box. "Is this the box" Gary showed the box to Henry. "Yes the pendant would be in this box".

When we opened the box, the scarab-shaped pendant was there on top of a book. Henry took out the pendant and the book. On the book it was written The Wilsons.

Henry opened the book and we saw his family photo. It was a family album. In the picture 4 persons were there and a little baby. "It's you, isn't it" I asked "Looks like you".

"Yes, it's probably me," Henry said. "Didn't she look like your mother? Who is she?" Gary asked, pointing to a young girl in the picture. "Yes, it looks like your mom" I agreed with Gary.

Is she her. She looks like her. "Henry... anyhow, do you know how old your mom is?" I asked Henry. "No, I don't...". "What..." Gary and I spoke simultaneously. "It can't possibly be her, can it, Finn?" Gary asked me. "It's impossible, that she is your mother". *I knew it... I knew she was too young to be Henry's Mom.* Henry was listening with his mouth opened. "What or Who is she?" Gary asked. "How would I know..." I replied. "Yes... it could be, I never saw my father" Henry replied. Henry seemed a bit worried. *Is this the Wilsons family secret? What's Henry thinkin' about now.*